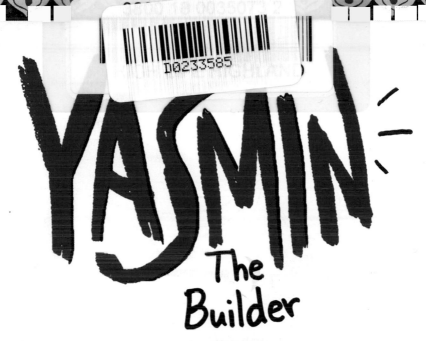

YASMIN

The Builder

written by
SAADIA FARUQI

illustrated by
HATEM ALY

raintree
a Capstone company — publishers for children

To Mariam for inspiring me, and
Mubashir for helping me find the
right words —S.F.

To my sister, Eman, and her amazing
girls, Jana and Kenzi —H.A.

Raintree is an imprint of Capstone Global Library Limited, a company
incorporated in England and Wales having its registered office at
264 Banbury Road, Oxford, OX2 7DY – Registered company number:
6695582

www.raintree.co.uk
myorders@raintree.co.uk

Text © 2019 Saadia Faruqi
Illustrations © 2019 Picture Window Books

Edited by Kristen Mohn
Designed by Aruna Rangarajan
Originated by Capstone Global Library Ltd
Printed and bound in India

ISBN 978 1 4747 6554 1
22 21 20 19 18
10 9 8 7 6 5 4 3 2 1

British Library Cataloguing in Publication Data
A full catalogue record for this book is available from the British
Library.

Acknowledgements
We would like to thank the following for permission to reproduce
design elements: Shutterstock: Art and Fashion, rangsan paidaen.

TABLE OF CONTENTS

CHAPTER 1

A new project

Ms Alex walked into the classroom with a big box.

"We are going to build a city today!" she announced.

The children were very curious. They all crowded around Ms Alex as she opened the box.

There were tubes and tape,

long sticks and round wheels.

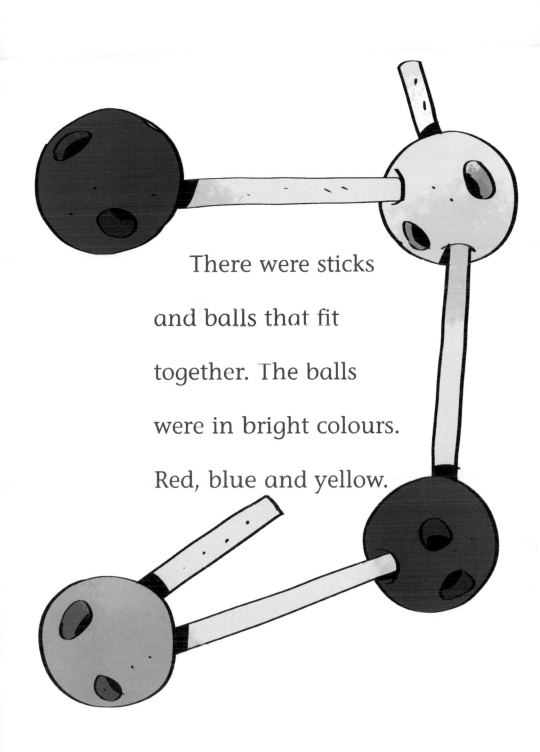

There were sticks
and balls that fit
together. The balls
were in bright colours.
Red, blue and yellow.

Yasmin watched as Ms Alex spread the building parts all over the carpet.

"When can we start?" Ali asked. He reached for a long stick.

"Not yet," replied Ms Alex. "First you will draw your idea on paper. That way you'll know what materials you will need."

"Boring!" said Ali.

Yasmin slowly pulled a piece of paper from her desk. She doodled. She sketched. She sighed.

How would these pieces on the

floor turn into a city? She didn't

know what to make. A roller

coaster? A hotel? A zoo?

CHAPTER 2

Get ready to build

Finally, Ms Alex told the children to begin building. "Think of everything a city has," she said. "Be creative!"

Ali was quick. In a few minutes, he built a castle.

"A castle in a city! I wish I'd

thought of that," Yasmin said.

Emma was slower. Her church was very tall and had a pointy steeple. "Now I need to make some people," Emma said.

Yasmin sat in the corner,

watching the others. She chewed

her lip. This was harder than she'd

thought.

"Yasmin, why aren't you

building something?" Ms Alex

asked.

"All the good ideas are already taken," Yasmin said.

"Well, what do you like doing best in the city?" Ms Alex replied.

Yasmin shrugged. "I like to go on walks. But you don't need to build anything for that."

Slowly Yasmin joined two long sticks together. Then two more. She had no idea what she was making. At least she looked busy.

CRASH!

Yasmin's stick tower fell down into a pile. She hid her face in her hands. What a mess.

CHAPTER 3

Connecting the dots

Soon, the bell rang for break.

"We can finish when we come back," said Ms Alex.

The children left, but Yasmin stayed behind. In the quiet room, she stared at the buildings. There was Ali's castle and Emma's church.

There was a school and three
houses. A tall building that looked
like a hotel. A supermarket and a
petrol station and a cinema.

And Yasmin's messy heap.

She could hear the other
children playing outside.

"We may go for a walk this afternoon," she heard Ms Alex call out.

That gave Yasmin an idea. She got to work, collecting all the leftover blocks and sticks and cardboard. She joined them together, here and there.

The bell rang just as she had finished. Everyone came back in.

Ms Alex was surprised.

"Yasmin, what's this?"

Yasmin smiled proudly.
"The buildings were lonely.
I joined them together with
pavements and bridges."

"Now the people can go on walks and visit each other!"

"Wonderful idea, Yasmin," said Ms Alex.

Emma said, "Hurray for Yasmin the bridge builder!"

Think about it, talk about it

* Yasmin has trouble coming up with an idea for the city her class is building. How do you come up with new ideas? What would you add to the city project if you could?

* What is your favourite thing about your town or city? What do you wish you could change?

* Think about a time you and a friend or classmate worked together on a project. Was it easier to come up with ideas when working with a partner?

Learn Urdu with Yasmin!

Yasmin's family speaks both English and Urdu. Urdu is a language from Pakistan. You may already know some Urdu words!

baba father

hijab scarf covering the hair

jaan life; a sweet nickname for a loved one

kameez long tunic or shirt

mama mother

naan flatbread baked in the oven

nana grandfather on mother's side

nani grandmother on mother's side

salaam hello

sari dress worn by women in South Asia

Pakistan fun facts

Yasmin and her family are proud of their Pakistani culture. Yasmin loves to share facts about Pakistan!

Location

Pakistan is on the continent of Asia, with India on one side and Afghanistan on the other.

Capital

Islamabad is the capital, but Karachi is the largest city.

Sport

The most popular sport in Pakistan is cricket.

Nature

Pakistan is home to K2, the second highest mountain in the world.

Build a castle with Yasmin and Ali!

SUPPLIES:

- shoebox
- construction paper of various colours
- scissors
- tape or glue
- felt-tip pens
- empty kitchen roll and toilet roll tubes, or other cardboard cylinders
- craft foam
- plastic straw or bamboo skewer

STEPS:

1. Wrap the shoebox with construction paper and tape it on. Draw on windows and a door. Stand the box upside down.

2. Cut paper to cover the assorted cardboard tubes/cylinders and tape on. Glue or tape them to the shoebox to make the castle towers.

3. Draw windows on the towers.

4. Make the roofs of the towers by cutting the craft foam into small cones and gluing them to the tops of the tubes.

5. Cut a flag from the construction paper and tape it to the straw or skewer. Glue your flagpole to a tower on your castle!

Saadia Faruqi is a Pakistani American
writer, interfaith activist and cultural
sensitivity trainer previously profiled
in *O Magazine*. She is author of the
adult short-story collection, *Brick Walls:
Tales of Hope & Courage from Pakistan*.
Her essays have been published in
Huffington Post, *Upworthy*, and *NBC
Asian America*. She lives in Texas, USA,
with her husband and children.

Hatem Aly is an Egyptian-born illustrator whose work has been featured in several publications worldwide. He currently lives in New Brunswick, Canada, with his wife, son and more pets than people. When he is not dipping cookies in a cup of tea or staring at blank pieces of paper, he is usually drawing books. One of the books he has illustrated is *The Inquisitor's Tale* by Adam Gidwitz, which won a Newbery Honor and other awards, despite Hatem's drawings of a farting dragon, a two-headed cat and stinky cheese.

Join Yasmin

on all her adventures!

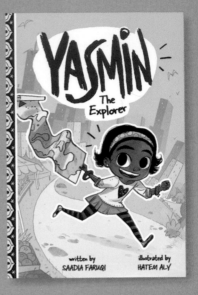

Discover more at

www.raintree.co.uk